You are fearfully and wonderfully made!

Linda Rossetti Brocato
Psalm 139:14

This book belongs to:

_____

Heart to Heart   Christian Books

Heart to Heart Publishing, Inc.
519 Muddy Creek Road ● Morgantown, KY 42261
(270) 526-5589
www.hearttoheartpublishinginc.com

Copyright © 2009 Linda Rossetti Brocato
Publishing Date January 2010
Library of Congress Control No. 2009938613
ISBN 978-0-9802486-1-6

Printed and Bound March 2010 in Nansha, Guangdong, China
by Everbest Printing Company, Ltd., through Four Colour Imports, Ltd., Louisville, Kentucky

Editor: Suzanne Nevins
Co-Editor: Evelyn Byers
Illustrator: Donna Brooks
Layout & Design: April Yingling

First Edition

Scripture Reference: NIV

Printed and Bound November 2009 (date of materials submission) in Nansha, Guangdong, China by Everbest Printing Company, Ltd., through Four Colour Imports, Ltd., Louisville, Kentucky.

Publisher's Cataloging-In-Publication Data
(Prepared by The Donohue Group, Inc.)

Brocato, Linda Rossetti.
   Ivan becomes a hero / by: Linda Rossetti Brocato ; illustrated by: Donna Brooks. -- 1st ed.

     p. : ill. ; cm.

   Summary: Tiny Baby Hillary the Hippo is missing. Neither Mother Hippo nor the other animals on the wildlife reserve can find her. Meanwhile, facing bullying and rejection, Ivan the Giraffe is learning that God made him special just the way he is, and he wants to help find Baby Hillary. When Scriptures touch his heart, Ivan becomes a brave voice.
   Interest age level: 003-008.
   ISBN: 978-0-9802486-1-6

1. Giraffe--Juvenile fiction. 2. Self-acceptance--Religious aspects--Christianity--Juvenile fiction. 3. Rejection (Psychology)--Religious aspects--Christianity--Juvenile fiction. 4. Giraffe--Fiction. 5. Self-acceptance--Fiction. 6. Rejection (Psychology)--Fiction. I. Brooks, Donna. II. Title.

PZ10.3.B7633 Iv 2010
[E]   2009938613

A letter to every parent, teacher, or caregiver:

All children wish to be valued, appreciated, and loved for who they are. Ivan is like a child. He is a little, gangly, curious giraffe with a deep longing to be accepted. Does this sound familiar? Yes, there is an Ivan in all of us! Thankfully, his wise mother knows the power of God's Word that imparts a sense of identity and adoption to Ivan, bringing him great joy. Psalm 139:14 is the Scripture to which I refer that Mother Giraffe reads to Ivan. Built on this simple truth, *Ivan Becomes a Hero* is a book that offers a life-changing message; one that heals hearts and emotions.

As adults, we have the awesome responsibility of fostering children in a safe and loving environment, namely our homes and classrooms. It is possible to protect and teach them, through God's Word, to value themselves as He values them. After reading this book I hope children will gain the freedom to express themselves and their own special praise to God for making them "one of a kind." Amazing!

I wish I had been so blessed when I was a child with this Scripture. But God's timing is perfect. He allowed me to feel the pain of shyness and loneliness. As a child I withheld my feelings. Now I am able to understand and share my experiences and blessings with children. I know I am "fearfully and wonderfully made!"

I believe children can learn compassion, acts of kindness in children lead to the same behavior as adults. Generosity is not only refreshing, but is God's will for us. When we look outside ourselves to the needs of others, all of us become heroes, sung or unsung. We reap the benefits of liking ourselves in a whole new way. Children love leaders who guide them so they may become all that God wants them to be. All children are "fearfully and wonderfully made!"

Help your child find the hidden hearts throughout the illustrator's artwork in this book. If you need help turn to the last page.

Words from a real-life Ivan...

When my mom started illustrating this story, I took a sneak peak at what she was doing. I read the story, and I realized I was an IVAN myself. As a child, I suffered from a condition called Tourettes Syndrome, a condition that leaves the person very much on the outside of everything. You feel unaccepted, teased, and like you are bad because something about you is different than others.

Just like Ivan, all I ever wanted was to be accepted and liked. But instead, I was tortured by their unkind words and deeds. I hope this book will make people see others as remarkable beings that God has designed for His purpose, and accept them for the wonderful people they are inside, not just the outside.

Remember - everyone has a special talent and reason for being just like Ivan. Everyone wants to be loved and accepted.

~ Brad Brooks

Dedications

I dedicate my first book to God, for giving me the inspiration
For Ivan Becomes a Hero,
The gift that allows me to teach children.

Also, to my husband, Frank Michael, my greatest encourager,
With my love.
Like Abraham, you "wavered not at the promise of God through unbelief;
But was strong in faith, giving glory to God." Rom. 4:20 (KJV)

And to my sons, Jason Michael and Stephen Matthew,
My daughter, Veronica Ann, by marriage to Jason Michael,
And my three grandchildren,
Rachel Moriah, Julia Orlit, and Jadon Michael,
How precious you are to me!

I could not have done this without each of you.

~ Linda Rossetti Brocato

I would like to dedicate this book to my precious little granddaughter, Abby Brooks. I hope and pray that she, nor any child, because of being different, would ever have to endure the pain of rejection such as Ivan had to endure.

~ Donna Brooks

Author Acknowledgements

I wish to acknowledge all of my sweet family and dear friends, including the Christian, Medical and Educational Communities who so lovingly supported me in prayers, love, and actions.

To all my former students – I have not forgotten you either!

Thank you to Linda J. Hawkins, publisher; Donna Brooks, illustrator; Suzanne Nevins, editor; April Yingling, designer; and Evelyn Byers, copy editor. I appreciate having worked with each of you personally in every aspect of Ivan's publication. I have learned so much as our talents merged and made Ivan special to children.

You will never know how much each of you touched my heart. Thank you!

Ivan Becomes a Hero

By: Linda Rossetti Brocato

Illustrated By: Donna Brooks

Ivan was a little giraffe who lived on a wildlife reserve. He loved to roam in his big backyard and play all day under the sunny skies.

At night, Ivan imagined
that he was the leader of
a grand parade, and all the
stars in the sky marched and
twinkled in step behind him. Even
though he was growing older, he still
liked to cuddle beside his mother under
the mighty mimosa tree as she read his favorite
Bible verse, Psalm 139:14 (NIV)

"I praise you (God) because I am fearfully
and wonderfully made; Your works are
wonderful, I know that full well."
Ivan felt the comfort of God's Word. He would gaze
into the shimmering sky and peacefully fall asleep.

One day, Ivan became curious about the world outside of his own backyard. He said, "I want to learn about this wide, wonderful world. I will visit the zebras in their backyard."

10

The zebras saw Ivan coming. They gazed at him from the horns atop his head to the hooves of his feet. They had NEVER seen anything so tall! Compared to Ivan they were short. He had orange giraffe spots. They had black zebra stripes. They said, "We do not like you because you do not look like us."

Zeke, leader of the zebras, crept behind Ivan and quickly bit off the fluffy tuft of his long tail! He no longer had a fluffy tuft to swish back and forth! Sadly, he galloped home.

Always close by, the nosy, babbling birds had been watching Ivan as he went on his new adventure. As soon as they saw what Zeke had done, they flew ahead of him to tell Mother Giraffe the sad news. **13**

Ivan's mother took one look at his tail and tried to encourage her little son. Ivan said, "Mother, I wish I were a zebra; then, I would be like them, and they would like me. I would have stripes, not spots. I would be short, not tall."

Ivan's mother looked at her tearful son and said, "Ivan, being a zebra would not make you happy. You are special the way God made you."

Mother Giraffe allowed him to play a little longer that night under the starry sky. When it was bedtime, she read his favorite Bible verse to him, explaining how fearfully and wonderfully God had created him.

The next day, Ivan became curious once again. "Phooey!" he said. "I don't care if the zebras don't like me. God loves me just the way I am! I wonder what the water buffaloes are like. Maybe they will become my friends!"

Cheerfully, Ivan ran to visit the water buffaloes in their backyard. They were splashing playfully and drinking from their watering hole. When they saw him coming, they began to laugh. "Ha! Ha! You are TOO tall!" the buffaloes jeered. "You cannot drink like we do!"

Ivan gathered what little confidence he had to try to drink like the buffaloes. He slid his l-o-n-g front legs further and further apart, and he leaned his l-o-n-g neck down until he could slurp the water easily with his l-o-n-g, purple tongue. The water buffaloes began to laugh and laugh. "We do not like you because you are not like us," they teased. "We do not look THAT silly when we drink water!"

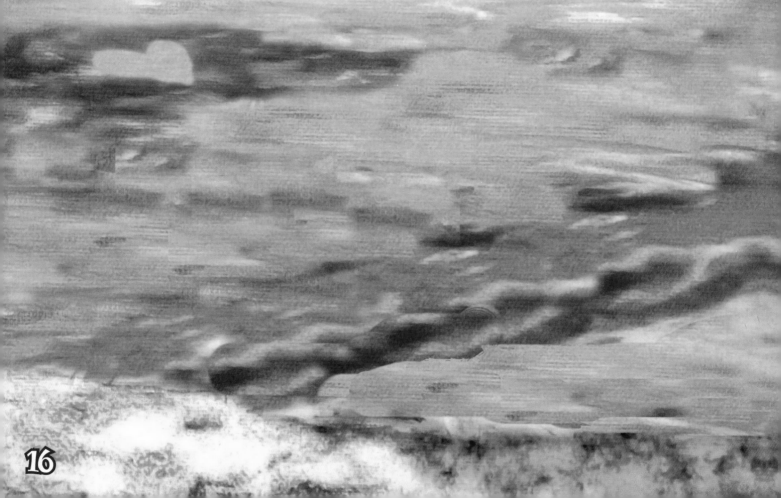

As the sun was setting, Ivan returned home in time for dinner. He was so unhappy his **l-o-n-g neck** was still hanging down.

Once again, the nosy, babbling birds had flown ahead of him and whispered the news of Ivan's encounter with the buffaloes in Mother Giraffe's ear.

Little Ivan was not hungry, so he went to bed early under the mighty mimosa tree. Mother Giraffe kissed him tenderly and opened the treasured Bible to comfort him. Ivan looked up at his mother with sad eyes. He said, "I wish I were a zebra, so I could have stripes and not spots. I want to be like them. Then, the zebras would like me and not make fun of me. I wish I were a water buffalo. Then, I could drink from their watering hole easily and splash and play like they do, and I would not look so silly."

Mother Giraffe said gently, "Ivan, always remember that God made you just the way you are for a purpose. There are a lot of things that YOU can do that the zebras and water buffaloes cannot do." Ivan was still thinking about his mother's wise words as he fell asleep.

The next morning, Ivan looked at the bright sunshine all around. He said to himself, "Phooey!

I'M IVAN THE CURIOUS GIRAFFE!

I LIKE WHO I AM BECAUSE GOD MADE ME IN A SPECIAL WAY!"

23

Ivan asked Mother Giraffe if he could visit Mrs. Hippo and her baby. "Sure, Ivan," she said. He raced gleefully to the hippo yard. He got there just in time.

Baby Hillary had disappeared suddenly without a trace, and no one could find her! Mrs. Hippo was very upset!

24

All the animal friends who came to help were quiet and sad. Ivan thought and thought. He began to pray. All of a sudden, a confident smile came across his face. "I can rescue Baby Hillary!" Ivan shouted. "I know I can!"

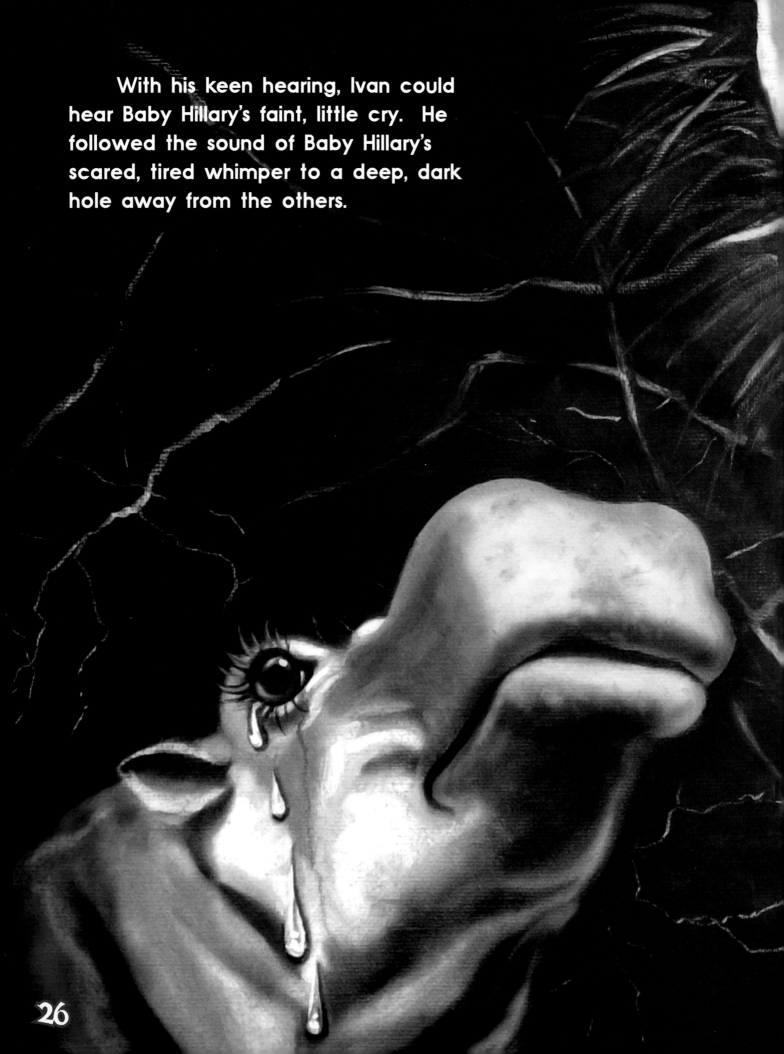

With his keen hearing, Ivan could hear Baby Hillary's faint, little cry. He followed the sound of Baby Hillary's scared, tired whimper to a deep, dark hole away from the others.

Slowly, Ivan knelt down on his front legs. Carefully, he stretched his l-o-n-g neck into the deep, dark hole. Baby Hillary, startled, looked up and suddenly stopped crying. She heard a calm voice say, "Hi, Hillary! I'm Ivan. Please, trust me ⁻ with GOD'S HELP, I have a plan to get you out of this hole ⁻ grab my l-o-n-g neck, and hang on tight!"

Carefully, Baby Hillary wrapped her tiny arms around Ivan's l-o-n-g neck. She held on tightly. In a few minutes, Ivan's l-o-n-g neck appeared from the deep, dark hole with a **BIG surprise! Baby Hillary was safe!** Gently, Ivan carried the tiny hippo to her grateful mother.

All the animal friends, even the nosy, babbling birds, cheered when Ivan brought Baby Hillary to her mother unharmed.

Baby Hillary gave Ivan her best "itsy-bitsy" hippo kiss, while Mother Hippo gave him a HUGE kiss! She said, "Ivan, can you see how special you are? You are brave and strong. I'm so glad that God gave you keen ears to hear, a l-o-n-g neck, and l-o-n-g legs, or my baby could have been eaten by a hungry lion.

YOU SAVED HER!
YOU ARE OUR HERO!"

Everyone had to agree that
Ivan was, indeed, a hero.

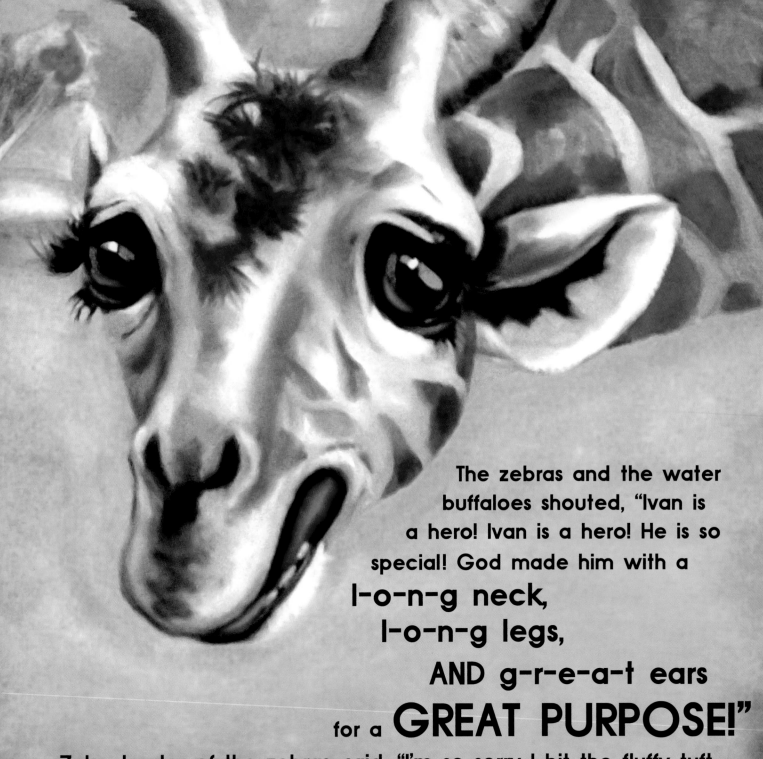

The zebras and the water buffaloes shouted, "Ivan is a hero! Ivan is a hero! He is so special! God made him with a l-o-n-g neck, l-o-n-g legs, AND g-r-e-a-t ears for a GREAT PURPOSE!"

Zeke, leader of the zebras, said, "I'm so sorry I bit the fluffy tuft off of your tail, Ivan. Please come to our yard and play tag anytime." Wally, leader of the water buffaloes, said, "Ivan, we're sorry we made fun of you, too. Can you find it in your heart to forgive us? You can drink and play in our watering hole anytime!"

Annie the Ape was standing by listening. She turned and said, "Look, Ivan. I don't even have a tail! You can be my new friend. Let's play Follow the Leader tomorrow with my friends, the monkeys."

A knowing grin came across Ivan's face as he remembered his favorite Bible verse. He declared, **"YES, I WILL PRAISE YOU, GOD, BECAUSE I AM FEARFULLY AND WONDERFULLY MADE, AND YOUR WORKS ARE WONDERFUL. I NOW KNOW THAT FULL WELL."** He smiled again when he remembered his mother's wise words to him, "There are many things you can do that the zebras and the water buffaloes cannot do."

With his MAGNIFICENT speed, he raced home to tell Mother Giraffe his good news! And this time -- the birds were happy for Ivan and allowed him to share his

Great, Grand Adventure!

Ivan shouted, "Mother, I rescued Baby Hillary today! She could have been eaten by a hungry lion! All my friends say that I am a hero! The zebras asked me to play tag with them. The water buffaloes invited me to drink and play in their watering hole. My new friend, Annie the Ape, wants to play Follow the Leader tomorrow. Mother, you were right. I am fearfully and wonderfully made by God!"

Ivan was filled with joy. He danced around and around in his wonderful backyard. He shouted,

"I am tall--not short!
I have spots--not stripes!
Yes, I have a l-o-n-g neck
and l-o-n-g legs.
And I have sharp ears, too.

Even though I have a tail that is no longer fluffy, I am

IVAN THE CURIOUS

who has become

IVAN THE BRAVE!

I am a **hero** because **God** made me just the way I am."

"I LIKE BEING ME!"

Ivan: A Blessed Vision to a Dream Come True

In the right time, visions and dreams are given to us as a beacon of light, guiding us with spiritual hope. Before he even had a name, Ivan was my beacon of light, his first rays revealed to me twelve years ago on a wildlife reserve. As I looked upon a newborn baby giraffe lying in the grass with Mother nearby, the infant Ivan was born in my heart. Quickly, I wrote the first words of what would later become Ivan Becomes a Hero on a small napkin. Little did I know how God would use this story to encourage me, along with many children, in the future.

With a strong, underlying passion for children, I returned to school and received my master's degree to continue teaching. However, after four short years in the classroom, that path was altered for me when I was diagnosed with cancer. Several years of chemotherapy, two transplants using my own stem cells, and the long process of restoring my health, only strengthened my reliance on God and my gratitude for His Grace. Just thankful for His Presence, He proceeded to remind me – I still had a way to minister to children – Ivan! I remembered I had a book to write! My beacon of light shone through the darkness.

As Ivan grew (on paper) and my health slowly returned, I still longed to care for children. God's promises continued to be fulfilled when my first granddaughter was placed in my arms. Oh! What a joy! And even more so when two more grandchildren followed. As God poured out His Grace, enabling me to care for them often, the story of Ivan became clearer, closer to full development. It lacked one thing: God's Word. Once Psalm 139:14 was centered into the story, it became the beautiful, bright light God wanted it to be.

Through love and trials, the story of Ivan has nurtured and been nurtured by many individuals, young and old, and is now given to countless children. May it encourage souls and stand as a symbol of God's faithful promises. My prayer is that you will open your heart and allow God to nurture you so your beacon of light, your dream, may be realized.

HEART ANSWERS:

6-7: on Ivan's shoulder
8-9: in sky
10-11: on Ivan's leg
12: Ivan's front right leg
13: between the two bottom birds in the blue sky
14: on Ivan's neck
15: on Ivan's chest
16-17: in the water
18-19: under the bird at Mother's ear, in the air swirls
20-21: on Ivan's lower neck
22-23: on Ivan's hip

24: in the throat of Mother Hippo
25: on Ivan's cheek
26-27: the hole
28: in the clouds on left
29: on Ivan's shoulder
30-31: on hippo's jaw
32-33: top of page, in green tree
34: on Ivan's neck
35: on Mother Giraffe's front leg up high
36-37: between Mother and Ivan, in green background
38: in the sky, upper right